For Marcus, Joshua, Astrid
and my sister Sandra who has always loved the blue bo

The narrative of
the second half of
the book
was created by
Jackie McKimmie,
who also gave valuable
assistance throughout
the book's development.

Come on, Crikey.

cut snipsnip
snippy snip
glue
cut snipsnip
snippy snip
glue

woof woof
woof woof

Run!
Run!
Big rain!
Big rain!
Whirly
wind!

woof woof woof

woof

Come on, Cat! Come on, Crikey! Here comes the storm!

We will
be
safe in
here.

Oil paint
on Cartridge
and Arches
paper
Water colour
Gouache
Pencils
Charcoal
Measuring
Tape
Stamp
Polka dot
Shirt
Band Aid
Wood

First published in Australia in 2014 by Allen & Unwin
First published in Great Britain in 2014 by Allen & Unwin

ISBN (AUS) 978 1 76011 003 1
ISBN (UK) 9 781 74336 363 8

10 9 8 7 6 5 4 3 2 1

This book was
printed in
April, 2014 at
Hang Tai Printing (Guang Dong) Ltd.,
Xin Cheng Ind Est,
Xie Gang Town,
Dong Guan,
Guang Dong Province,
China

A Cataloguing-in-Publication entry
is available from the
National Library of Australia
www.trove.nla.gov.au and from the
British Library.

© Words and images
2014
Chris McKimmie
Thank you
again,
Erica
and
Susannah

Book design, cover design,
lettering by
Chris McKimmie

Allen & Unwin – Australia
83 Alexander St
Crows Nest
NSW
2065
Australia
Phone: (61 2) 8425 0100
Email: info@allenandunwin.com
Web: www.allenandunwin.com

Allen & Unwin – UK
c/o Murdoch Books
Erico House
93-99 Upper Richmond Road
London SW 15 2TG
Phone: 020 8785 5995
Email: info@murdochbooks.co.uk
Web: www.allenandunwin.com
Murdoch Books is a wholly owned division
of Allen & Unwin Pty Ltd.